Our Little Quebec Cousin

Mary S. Saxe

Our Little Quebec Cousin

CHAPTER I

AN INTRODUCTION

THE traveler who comes to visit on the island of Montreal gets no correct idea of the beauty of it all until he has climbed to the top of Mount Royal, which rises directly behind the great city of Montreal in the Province of Quebec. From this elevation, about one thousand feet above sea level, the observer beholds not only the banks of the St. Lawrence river, with its warehouses, grain elevators and shipping; he sees not only this solidly built city of churches—but far to his left stretches the farming country of the Province of Quebec, far to his right, on clear days he can see the Adirondack Mountains and Lake Champlain, while on the opposite shores of the St. Lawrence, spanned by the once famous Victoria Bridge, he sees the villages of Longueil and St. Lambert.

Then, from the very summit of this mountain, he must also look behind him and see the numerous small towns and villages that lie back of Mount Royal, all of these being reached by tramways which run out from Montreal.

The largest of these settlements are known, one as Outremont, the other as Cote-des-Neiges; translated into English these would be known as "behind the mountain" and "hill of snow."

It was in the latter village of Cote-des-Neiges that little Oisette Mary Tremblent, our little Canadian, or, rather, our little Quebec cousin, was born. The French Canadian child is the product of five generations of French people whose ancestors came from France with Champlain and Jacques Cartier, and who, when the British won Canada from France, were allowed by the British to keep their own tongue, their own religion and their own flag.

Let me introduce Oisette Mary Tremblent, our little Quebec cousin, to you. Behold, then, a very plump little girl, with skin the color of saffron tea and a nose as flat as flat can be. There never were such bead-like eyes, nor such black shiny hair as hers.

She usually wore a black and red checked dress of worsted, with bright blue collar and cuffs, and around her neck was a purple ribbon, on which was hung a silver medal. On this medal was stamped the figure of the Blessed Virgin Mary.

It will be seen that Oisette Mary's people loved gay colors.

She was a very happy little girl from the time she slipped out of bed in the morning, always awakened by the neighboring church bell of the parish ringing its three strokes — "Father, Son and Holy Ghost." When she heard this bell, Oisette bowed her little head three times and made the sign of the Cross.

Her day was thirteen hours long and she knew no naps! Small wonder that she fell asleep the moment her head touched the pillows, and she heard nothing of the violin playing, the singing and sometimes dancing that went on in the rooms below stairs.

Oisette Mary had two older sisters away at a convent school, two older brothers, one already studying for the priesthood, and one small baby brother, who spent long hours on the cottage floor with "Carleau" the dog, for company.

A family of six children! What a large family you think? Not at all! French Canadian families frequently number twelve or more, and less than ten children is counted as a small household.

Monsieur Tremblent, Oisette's father, owned a large and valuable melon patch. You know Montreal melon is famous the world over; and on fine days in August one could see Monsieur Tremblent walking slowly along, counting his melons as they grew.

"Un, deux, trois, quatre," he would murmur. In his wake little Oisette would follow, gay little parrot that she was, also repeating after him. "Cinque, six, sept, huit." In this way she had learned to count.

Now, it happened that the tenth melon was a large fine one, and, when Oisette beheld it, she sat right down beside it, put her two little arms around it and murmured: "C'est pour Monsieur, le Curé," which translated into English reads: "This is for the priest." Her father chuckled and said to

Louis, her brother, who was weeding hard by, "She is just like her mother, the little one, she always remembers the priest."

Madame Tremblent was diminutive in stature, her two interests in life were her home and her church; she understood the English language as she heard it spoken, but she had never attempted to utter a word in English herself, nor could she read a line of anything but French.

Her husband wore a silk hat and frock coat on Sundays and Holy Days, he attended political meetings and was a keen politician, could address a meeting in either tongue, as can most young Canadian Frenchmen; but Madame apparently took no interest other than to see that her husband's coat was well brushed, his silk hat very glossy indeed.

She consulted her priest when anything worried her, she had so little faith in banks that she always carried her house-keeping money either in her stocking or in her petticoat pockets.

There came a day in early September when quantities of melons were gathered for the market, put in the big farm wagon, and Oisette was allowed to sit by her father on the high seat as they drove to the Bonsecour Market in Montreal. The start was made in the early morning. Oisette sang to herself as they rumbled along.

"Alouette, gentille Alouette, Alouette, Je te plumerai,

Je te plumerai la tête, Je te plumerai la tête,

O Alouette, gentille Alouette, Alouette, Je te plumerai."

The French Canadian is apt to sing when he is very happy, and Oisette was especially happy to-day, for she knew that that tenth melon, or one very like it, had been left in the front vestibule of her home, ready to be sent to the priest's home later in the day.

There is one quality that the French Canadian child has, which is not always to be found in children of every nationality: namely, obedience. One seldom finds a naughty or willful little French boy or girl. They are stolid perhaps and placid, but there is no kicking or screaming.

On this particular September morning, Oisette, when the Bonsecour Market was finally reached, waited patiently for her father, she sat on the high seat now by herself. The team, along with many others, was lined up beside the market. From this perch she could see the beautiful river, the boats coming in and leaving the harbor; she could see the wharves and the loading and unloading of great steamers. It was all very fascinating.

Then back of her was the great market, all the stalls were piled high with fruit and vegetables of every size and shape in a riot of color.

Along the pavement were coops of live chickens and turkeys. There were long pouches of "black pudding," dangling from the booths. The stalls were heaped with home grown tobacco, dark slabs of maple sugar, home woven toweling, curtains, rugs, carpets, firmly knit socks, elaborately plaited mats. A charm and a glamor hangs over the generally commonplace business of buying and selling, getting gain, and making provision for the needs of the day. The whole thing is like a gay picture book. There are groups of habitant women, all talking in chorus; the queer little blue and red carts that have come from across the river by ferry; the small pink pigs squealing their hardest as they are lifted from the crates of the vendors to the sacks of the purchasers; the squawking of fowls whose end is near. Certainly Bonsecour Market is a spot to be visited if one would see the Habitant in his happiest mood.

About ten o'clock the customers arrive. There are lovely ladies in limousines, and sometimes there would hop out of a motor a prettylittle English Canadian girl, to buy some nuts from open bags which always stand in rows along the pavements.

One day a very lively little missie gave Oisette a handful of English walnuts and invited her to climb down and come inside the market and see some little pigs.

But Oisette had been told to remain on guard, and remain she did. Now and then she would have a glimpse of her father as he went from stall to stall disposing of his stock.

One of his best customers was an old Irish dame, who had a French name because she had married in her youth one Alphonse LeBlanc, but she did not speak French at all. She was very popular with the English customers, and many of the "quality" (as she called them), bought her fruit and vegetables because she spoke their tongue. Her manners, too, made her famous throughout the market. As a customer arrived, she would make a deep curtsy, as though Royalty approached, and would say in her rich brogue, "And what fer yez, Darlin?"

One market day, when a cold slanting rain came on, Madame LeBlanc insisted that Monsieur Tremblent should lift little Oisette down and bring her inside Madame's stall.

So she was made very cozy beside a diminutive stove, known as a Quebec heater. It certainly was a very warmth giving stove, with a black iron kettle on the top, which poured forth a long plume of white steam. On a shelf hard by a big yellow and black cat purred very loud, as though trying to beat the kettle. He was flanked on each side by pyramids of cheese.

In spite of wind and weather, customers arrived, one and two at a time; they would step inside one at a time, leaving just room enough for Madame to curtsy. Most of them noticed Oisette and asked Madame about her. When Monsieur Tremblent came back at last to call for his little girl, he found she had made friends with the cat and had her pockets full of latire (molasses candy), and was holding a big red apple. Small wonder that her face was wreathed in smiles.

When her father opened the door, Oisette heard Madame say: "Come in, dear, shut the door, and we'll have a cup of tay."

A cup of this strong brewing was prepared for little Oisette as a matter of course — which may explain why her complexion was so murky.

On this particular market day however, as she sat beside her father, the fresh September breeze gave her a very bright color, and her eyes were shining with excitement. Several lovely things had happened, all of which she would remember to tell her mother about when home was reached. First there was a band of music leading some fine-looking soldier boys along the road, and the tune was very catching. The boys were all singing "Over There" as they swung along. Then, because some road was closed for repairs, her father had driven into town by a new route and she saw, for the first time, a statue of the late King Edward the Seventh, which she admired very much. Then after the big market wagon rumbled down a very steep long hill, she saw the monument in Place d'Armes Square known as "The Landing of Maisonneuve."

This was an old friend, but she was never tired of looking at it, and knew all the figures about the base. There was the fierce Iroquois Indian crouching for his prey. There was the huntsman with his gun and dog; there was the sweet-faced nun, Jeanne Mance, who founded the order of Black Nuns in Canada, and then, atop of all, was the dashing French Cavalier Maisonneuve in his plumed hat, corselet and top boots. He was the founder of this great city of Montreal in the year 1642.

She was never tired of hearing the story of those early days as her father told it to her.

How the brave voyageurs had come to a land filled with hostile tribes of Indians. First these adventurous Frenchmen settled in Quebec, the city of Quebec was founded, and then Paul de Comedy, Sire de Maisonneuve, being anxious to follow up this great river St. Lawrence, coaxed his men to row with him the one hundred and sixty miles right against a swift current until they came to Mount Royal and beheld the swift rapids in the river; these are now called Lachine Rapids. So they decided to land and build another village.

One can read in Parkman's history a very clear picture of that scene, just at twilight when they stepped from their boats and tired as they were, they stopped to build an altar and hold a mass of thanksgiving to God for the safe journey. For lights on that altar, they imprisoned fireflies in bottles and the company all knelt on the ground while the mass was said. They were watched by hostile Iroquois Indians who lurked in the shadow of the trees.

All this was long long ago. There are no more Indians wearing blankets nowadays. But on this spot where mass was said rises the great solid city of

Montreal with its two nationalities, French and English, trying to live in harmony.

This statue stands in Place d'Armes Square, just in front of the famous Notre Dame church, with its twin towers, two hundred and twenty-seven feet high. In these towers hang some famous chimes. One bell of this chime weighs twenty-four thousand seven hundred and eighty pounds and is known as the Great Bourdon. It takes seven men to ring it, and it has a deep booming note that is heard for miles.

There is a legend about this corner of the square where this church stands. It seems that there is always a breeze blowing just here,even the very hottest day in summer, and the story goes that on this corner the Devil and the Wind once met, and the wind as it swept up from the river and swirled around the corner said to the Devil: "I'll travel along with you," and Satan replied, "Before we start, I must go into this great church here and confess my sins, so you wait around this corner until I am done." And the wind said: "Very well, I'll hang around." Now, when the Devil got into the confessional, he had so many sins to confess that he is still there, and the wind still waits on that corner; waiting, waiting.

One day when Oisette Mary drove past that street corner, the wind did sweep up through the narrow street, from the river, swirl around the corner and away went her hat rolling across the square, driven by the summer breeze until it was caught at the base of the Maisonneuve monument and finally handed back to her by a French boy. So she never forgot the legend.

CHAPTER II

TWO WONDERFUL EVENTS

ONE Saturday afternoon, in fact the very next day after the market trip, Oisette's father could have been seen walking through the village street; he was carrying under his arm that tenth melon, or one very like it, which his daughter had selected for the Curé.

In his wake came our little Quebec cousin, her red ribbons bobbing along. Carleau, the dog, was at her heels, his short tail, as he walked, moved like the rudder on a boat.

This village street, with its white plaster houses and rows of poplar trees, was very picturesque. There was a yellow sunlight tipped over everything. Just as this little procession crossed the dusty road to enter the rectory gate, a big motor came purring along. In the tonneau were two ladies and a dear little girl; the latter had flying yellow curls.

"MR. SAGE . . . WAS WAVING A GREENBACK IN MONSIEUR TREMBLENT'S FACE"

"Pappa," she called, "see the big melon!" Now pappa was at the wheel, driving his own car. He was watching the road carefully; he had fears lest the little French girl might suddenly dart in front of the car; he had also observed Carleau, but the melon was the one thing in the foreground that he had missed; and, strange to say, a melon was the very thing these people had set out to find.

So, in the twinkling of an eye, the big car was brought to a full stop and Mr. Sage, its owner, was waving a greenback in Monsieur Tremblent's face.

Mr. Sage was naturally a silent man, his motto was "Money talks." Therefore he was somewhat amazed that the owner of the melon did not hand the fruit to him at once; and still more surprised was he to see Oisette Mary give one of her funny little bows and hear her say: "Pardon Monsieur, c'est pour Monsieur le Curé," and then she added in English "but there are many more chez moi."

The ladies laughed in chorus and repeated, "Many more at your house, then jump right in and show us the way."

"More as good as that one, eh?" asked Mr. Sage, as he opened the car door.

Monsieur Tremblent was dumb with surprise, he had been inclined to accept the offer and turn back to get another melon for the Curé, but Oisette won the day by jumping into the car. "I always have good luck," he told his priest afterward, "when I take the little one."

Those people not only bought three melons, but promised to come again.

When Oisette Mary was eight years of age two very wonderful events occurred, which events stood out in her memory for all time.

One was when she took her first communion in the month of May, which all good Catholics know as the month of Mary; and the second was at the end of that same year, on Christmas Eve, when she was allowed to attend the midnight mass with her parents for the first time.

"BERNADETTE . . . LOOKED UP"

Little girls who take their first communion are such a pretty sight, for they are all dressed in white; white stockings, white slippers, dress and veil and around their heads each one has a wreath of white flowers.

The church service is always early in the day. Oisette's communion was given at a picturesque little church in the East End of Montreal. This church is known as Notre Dame de Lourdes. (Our Lady of Lourdes.) It is a copy of the larger church at Lourdes, France, and over the high altar is a representation of a little girl kneeling before an image of the Blessed Virgin Mary. Almost a century ago there was a little girl in Lourdes, France, named Bernadette, who being sent one morning very early to a grotto, by her parents, was told to bring home a pitcher of spring water from the clear spring that bubbled there, and the legend was that when Bernadette knelt to catch the water she looked up and saw, high on a rock in the grotto, the figure of the Blessed Virgin Mary, and the Virgin smiled at her and told her that the water had a healing power. Ever since that time many pilgrims have visited Lourdes in France and been healed by its waters.

Certainly the little church in Montreal has a decided charm. Directly a visitor enters he observes over the high altar the figure of little Bernadette kneeling in her blue dress and white cap and above her is the figure of the Virgin. Lights above the Virgin's head are so arranged that a most beautiful glow falls upon her face and figure. Children all love this little church, and it is a pretty sight to see them marching through its portals two and two. The small boys look well in black suits, white collars and white ribbons tied on the left arm. But they get little attention, admiration all being centered on the dainty little maidens about to make their first communion.

When the service is over, these little communicants wear their white garb all day long, and go about visiting all their relatives and friends until nightfall. At each household they visit they expect a gift, sometimes it is a rosary or a prayer book, or a locket, and sometimes it is money put in the shoe for luck.

Oisette's day ended with a drive out to Bord a Plouffe, near the end of the Island of Montreal, where the Sacred Heart Convent is to be found. Here she visited her two older sisters who were at school. She heard the children sing "Stella Maris," she watched a procession about the grounds, little girls making a "Novena," and she had a glass of milk and some cake. Best of all, one of the nuns gaveher a lovely little silk banner with the figure of Joan of Arc woven on it. This she took home and hung on her bedroom wall. It became one of her very dearest possessions.

The midnight mass as celebrated at the Notre Dame Cathedral in Montreal is a sight no one can forget. About eleven on the night before Christmas, the wonderful chime of bells sends out its clamor on the frosty air. "Chim-Chime, Chim-Chime"—they sound from out the high twin towers, and when the Great Bourdon sounds the note in its deep throat the notes carry many miles. It is not sounded every day, but for weddings, funerals and on great church festivals, and its tones are heard above the noise of trolley cars, sleigh bells and other street traffic. On Christmas Eve these chimes are heard by the tired Christmas shoppers, and the still more weary shop girls, and the streams of people on their way home from the theaters. Little Oisette, in a warm velvet coat, a red toque on her head and a red knitted scarf wound around her waist, long red stockings pulled on over her boots, and rubbers put over these stockings, was lifted into the family sleigh and tucked well under the buffalo robes—she could still see the sky, full of wonderful stars, and she could hear, even through her toque, which was well over her ears, the booming of the Great Bourdon.

"THEY DROVE INTO THE CITY"

She liked the way the snow squeaked under the runners of the sleigh, she liked the way the big farm horses kicked the snow, she liked the way the evergreen boughs, loaded with snow, held out their branches toward her.

There is nothing more comfortable than one of these Canadian sleighs full of robes; they are built low on runners close to the ground, and they have a high back which keeps off the wind. The whole effect is somewhat like a wooden bathtub on runners; the seats are wide enough to hold a whole family.

How proud our little Quebec cousin felt to be riding with her father, her mother, her two sisters and two brothers! Her cheeks grew red and redder with the thrill of it. There were hot bricks in the bottom of the sleigh to keep her mother's feet warm, her two sisters held hot potatoes in their muffs. The French Canadian knows how to conserve heat. Long before the day of Thermos bottles and fireless cookers he heated bricks and stones, and sealed up the windows of his home against all wintry blasts. It is a very stuffy atmosphere they breathe, but there is so much latent heat stored in their bodies that they can take a long drive, if well muffled, without the chill of the weather penetrating their bones.

Oisette Mary's eyes grew round and rounder with surprise as they drove into the city and she saw the blaze of electric signs for the first time. The portals of the great church looked very gloomy in comparison until they entered the church, and then she saw for the first time the high altar, with its splendor of colored lights. It is a sight to take the breath away. Tall candles, short candles, clusters of red, green, blue, yellow lights all twinkling like stars; and the organ playing delightful music.

Her father picked Oisette up in his arms, and they went down a long side aisle to visit the manger of the Infant Christ. There it was, very lifelike indeed; piles of straw, heads of cattle, the Infant Christ in wax was lying in some straw, and there were kneeling figures of Joseph and Mary by its side.

After a while Oisette and her father were seated in a pew very close to the chancel and she could see the priests, nineteen in all, who waited on the archbishop; then the little acolytes, six in number, who waited on the priests, were a pretty sight. The organ played "Adeste Fidelis." Then the mass began. The incense poured up in volumes toward the groined roof. At last Oisette fell asleep on "bote of de eye," as the French Canadian would express it, and she never awakened until they were traveling homeward again.

"Do you know where you are, little one?" asked the father, as he cracked his whip. "I am on the front seat with mon père," she replied with a sleepy smile, and curled up again like a little dormouse.

Now one would imagine that when her home was reached, Oisette Mary would, before going to bed, hang up her stocking and prepare for a visit from Santa Claus; or even — it being about two o'clock in the morning — that she might find he had already filled her stocking or decked a Christmas tree for her delight.

Not a bit of it! The French Canadian child does not give nor does she receive gifts on Christmas Day. For these people the day is simply a religious festival; a holy day rather than a holiday.

So Oisette Mary, at two o'clock in the morning of Christmas Day, was given a bowl of hot pea soup, with plenty of onion in it — and put to bed.

CHAPTER III

NEW YEAR'S DAY

"SOME OF THE BOYS ARRIVING ON SNOWSHOES BROUGHT FRIENDS WITH THEM"

NEW Year's Eve in the Province of Quebec is quite another story; when that time arrived Oisette Mary was allowed to keep very late hours. Her brothers and sisters were all at home; some of the boys arriving on snowshoes brought friends with them.

A fiddler came (one could hardly call him a violinist). He sat on a chair which had been placed on a table; from this platform he called the dances and played his fiddle and beat time with his foot and sometimes, too, he sang to the music, and so did all the company. It was an orgy of sound.

Oisette kept awake until after supper; she was allowed a generous slice of an especially prepared cake known as "gillete du beurre" which the well-to-do Habitant serves to his guests at this season. Her pockets were full of nuts and raisins, and she was holding a new doll in her arms. As they arrived, every one kissed her on both cheeks, as is the French custom, and every one called out "Heureux Année" to her; which is their way of saying "Happy New Year."

During the festivities, the village Curé came in to call. He stood and watched the dancing and applauded the musician. He also shook hands with each member of the family and their guests. He sang with them, feasted with them, and smoked with the men. He was a very lovable character and had a wonderful power for good among his people. He brought Oisette a box of figs as a New Year's offering, and he patted her on the head when at last she went away to bed. The Curé went home at midnight, but the party went on until dawn.

The following morning, when Oisette awoke from her slumbers, she saw on the windowsill a little sparrow hopping about on the snowy ledge, so she tossed back the quilts, and ran down to her mother to beg for some crumbs.

To her surprise all her family objected, until it was explained to her by her father, that, according to a superstition that the French Canadian holds, no person should be allowed to carry anything out of a house on New Year's Day until something fresh has been brought in.

So she stood, with a tin biscuit box in her hand, in which were a lot of crumbs, waiting until some one should enter the outside door. It was very hard work for her to wait, and the bird seemed very impatient, but the family had said no, and when those who are older say no, it does not do to disobey. The French Canadian child is naturally obedient.

Presently she was rewarded and her tears turned to smiles, for with much scraping and pounding the outer door opened and in came her Uncle Napoleon, his arms filled with an assortment of packages.

Now, Napoleon was a guest of honor, for he was a young priest, and had but recently returned from the city of Baltimore, in the United States, where he had been in retreat. He, too, kissed all his relatives on both cheeks, as he distributed his gifts. When he came to little Oisette he put in her hand a small box, the top of which was full of small holes. "Have a care, little one," he said, "for your gift is alive."

Oisette was so thrilled that she let her tin box drop with a bang, crumbs and all. "Is it a mouse?" she ventured, "or a bird, mon oncle?"

Napoleon laughed and shook his head. "This box will make a good home for it," he said. "If we find some sand, some stones andsome water." "It is a fish then!" declared her father, only he called it "un poisson."

In the meantime the little girl placed the package on the table and opened it carefully. "Oh — oo! la-la," she said, as out walked, very, very slowly, a baby turtle — just two inches long from tip to tip.

There were directions with it, from the vicar at St. Remo, explaining that it was full size and would need a little water to live in, a few crumbs and flies to live on.

So with stones taken from a flower pot, and sand from a celery box, a nice home was made inside the tin biscuit box.

On an island or dock formed by the stones and a bit of wood, the little turtle came out to sun himself when tired of the water. It was amusing, indeed, to watch him study his own image which was reflected in the side of the tin box. This tin, you see, was as clear and bright as a mirror, and to watch him bob his head about as he stopped to reflect on his new estate made the whole family laugh like children.

His little mistress wanted to call him "Vanity," but her Uncle Napoleon told her that the good vicar of St. Remo had named him "Jean Batiste," which is the French for John the Baptist!

Oisette was a tender-hearted little girl and she did not long forget that there were some little birds out in the cold dooryard, waiting for her to feed them. "Now, you see," she explained to her uncle, "since you have entered our house and brought in a turtle, I can carry out some crumbs to the poor oiseaux,—and, I suppose," she mused, "it means that we shall have turtles coming in all the year since a turtle was the first thing brought in on the glad New Year's Day."

Her Uncle Napoleon laughed very hard at this philosophy, and said: "But I should think the milk was brought in the first thing veryearly this morning, was it not, little one? Certainly you will have milk all the year, will you not?"

"Yes," chimed in her father. "We must thank the Bon Dieu that we shall have milk all the year."

Why had they not thought of that sooner, Oisette wondered, and not kept the birds waiting all this time! She could hear them now, chirp, chirp, chirp as though to hurry her.

Just at that moment Jean Batiste put his head out and winked solemnly and Oisette Mary opened the outer door and threw out plenty of crumbs; so it would seem that everybody and everything about the Tremblent farm had a Happy New Year.

CHAPTER IV

NEW NEIGHBORS

THAT January an English-speaking family rented a house right next to the Tremblent home. Oisette watched them as they moved in, with the greatest interest; she soon discovered that there were two girls and a smaller boy. The boy seemed to be about her own age.

As soon as they were settled, their governess came out from the city of Montreal, on a tram car, to teach them each morning. Oisette learned also to watch for her appearance.

Then, when the mysterious lessons were over, the pupils, well bundled in very warm clothing, would escort their governess to the trolley station; after that they were free to play out in the beautiful snow all the day long.

They built a huge snow fort to keep out the Indians, which the boy insisted still lurked in the woods back of Mount Royal. They built a snow house to live in, a room for each one of them, and an extra room for guests, since there was plenty of snow; and, last of all, they started a wonderful snow man, which was to stand on guard at the house door.

At first Oisette was terribly shy about playing with them, but they were inclined to be friendly with her and even tried to talk in the French tongue with her, for their governess had told them to do so. When finally they saved a bone every day for Carleau, so that he spent most of his daylight hours in holding the fort for them, and when they begged Oisette to show them her turtle, she was won over.

And after a week or so she boldly showed them how to improve their snow man by marking his face with lumps of charcoal for eyes, red flannel for lips, an old pipe stuck in his mouth, and a very battered old hat of her father's on his head, she became their strongest ally. In fact she received so much praise from the Dudley family that she became quite embarrassed. However, she learned to call them all by their baptismal names. Such good sturdy English names they were. The boy was George Howard Dudley, he being named for King George of England of course, and the elder girl was Alexandra May after the Dowager Queen and present queen of England,

and the younger was called Victoria after her own grandmother, who, in her time, had been named after Queen Victoria, who reigned over the British Empire so many, many years. This younger little Dudley girl was always called "Queenie," which name Oisette thought was very beautiful indeed.

One day they were all out tobogganning together on the hillside when a funeral procession passed along the road below. As the hearse appeared in sight little Oisette stopped in her play and crossed herself; the others, after a moment, stopped their shrill screaming too, and waited respectfully.

One of the children who was sliding on the hillside that morning was a little American cousin from Plattsburgh, New York; being a newcomer, she had never before seen a hearse just like this one.

It was white all over, runners and body and harness, and on the four corners of this hearse were figures made in white plaster; these figures represented kneeling angels, and they had gold tipped wings and were holding long gold trumpets to their lips. In the center of the top of this vehicle was an upright gilt cross and from it floated long streamers of white, these flapped in the chill wind.

Three sleigh loads of mourners followed, and though they had black crepe streamers tied to their fur caps, they did not appear mournful at all, for the men were smoking pipes and chatting together, and they all leaned out to look at the snow man which the children had constructed.

Among the well-to-do French Canadian families in the Province of Quebec, a white hearse and a white casket is always used for the burial of a child. If they cannot afford this, they simply hire "a rig" as they call it; and put as many of the family on the rear seat as the space will allow, and on the front seat sits the father and drives the horse, while in his lap he holds the tiny white coffin, and in it is the body of the little dead child. Many, many of these primitive funeral processions pass along the Cote-des-Neiges Road to the Roman Catholic Cemetery which lies behind the mountain—for the infant mortality in this particular province is very, very heavy.

On Saturdays, and on Sunday afternoons, too, this road takes a more cheerful aspect, when hundreds of boys and girls arrive on snow shoes, or come in long sleighs, dragging toboggans behind them, for these hills back of Mount Royal are a splendid winter playground. Almost every winter there is a ski-jumping contest, when some wonderful athletes come from Norway and other Northern countries to compete with these young Canadian athletes.

Then, too, there are young Frenchmen who love to race their horses, sometimes they practice the speed of a mare along these roads, and then some beautiful Sunday afternoon they take part in horse races along the river road.

In wintertime it is so very cold that the great St. Lawrence river is frozen solid, and all day long traffic is driven over this ice from shore to shore. From the top of Mount Royal one can distinctly see the road which leads from the city of Montreal to a good-sized town on the south shore known as Longueil. This road is marked by little evergreen trees which have been cut from the forest and placed along either side of the roadway, to mark the path when dusk draws on. It is a very picturesque sight to watch this river road on a busy morning, when one can see a procession of red or blue box sleighs, each one being driven by a Habitant farmer, who sits on his bags of potatoes and onions and pork, and jogs along very comfortably toward the great city.

Once every winter Monsieur Tremblent would drive his fine team of horses over from Montreal to Longueil by the river road to call on some of his political friends and that year he allowed little Oisette to go with him, and she begged to take the little Dudley girls with her, so they were all wrapped up with extra care and cuddled down among the robes on the rear seat, and when it was too late to send him back, it was discovered that Carleau had followed them when they left the island of Montreal and started out on the wide river'sfrozen surface. The little Dudleys were just a little nervous at first, but they saw so many teams in front of them going toward the opposite shore that at last they forgot about the great river which lay under the frozen road.

This shore at first looked like a thin blue line; by and by it began to look like a wall, and at last the children could see roads and houses and churches, and when they looked back there was the great city of Montreal, which they had left; now it looked like a thin blue line.

Carleau caused some excitement by chasing off after another dog, and leaving the prescribed route. They had to stop the horses and call "Carleau, Carleau, mauvais chien," to coax him back again. When he did return, he was told to jump into the sleigh and lie down under the robes, at the children's feet. Once in a while, if the sleigh gave an extra bump, he would give a short bark, but it was hardly noticed at all above the jingle of sleigh bells, the laughter of the children and the squeak of the runners over the ice.

On each side of this road enterprising business men have placed advertisements, printed both in English and in French. The Dudley children found great delight in reading these aloud; for already their governess had taught them to read and to spell very well indeed.

Our little Quebec cousin had to maintain a discreet silence, for she had never been to school and could not yet read either French or English. On Sundays she recited her catechism to the Curé, and in another year's time she would go to a convent, to be educated by the nuns, as her older sisters were now being taught.

Fortunately, Monsieur Tremblent could well afford to educate his children, but there are many French Canadians who never learn to read nor write, because education is not free in this province and is not compulsory. Is this not a very sad condition of things to exist in a Christian country in the twentieth century! But we must not blame these people individually. Remember, it is the government which controls such matters. Oisette had a quick mind and sharp eyes and by listening to the chatter of these English tongues she picked up a great deal of information.

Each morning, all that winter, our little Quebec cousin waited patiently for her playmates to finish their lessons, and be ready to come out and play with her. She had been told that she must wait and not disturb them, so she sat all hooded and cloaked by her cottage window until she heard their voices. The French Canadian child certainly has two good traits, Obedience and Patience.

When her neighbors finally came trooping out, she would open her own door with one of her slow smiles and call out "Bon Jour, mes amis," and then Carleau, who had waited just as patiently as his little mistress, would rend the air with barks and yelps of joy, and the wonderful playtime would commence.

While the snow still lies deep in the woods, but the March winds and sunshine are causing the sap to rise in the trees, comes the magical time in the Province of Quebec, known as "Maple Sugar Time." In early days the Indians, who then inhabited this land, tapped his trees aslant with a tomahawk and inserted above this opening a strip of wood or pipe from which the sap fell drop by drop into a birch bark receptacle. This sap was boiled in earthenware vessels. In this way they obtained a quantity of thick black syrup, the only sugar used by the Indians. As the sap was always boiled in the open, bits of bark fell into it and it had a smoky taste. But about fifty years ago, this maple sugar industry was more carefully looked after, and nowadays the well-to-do farmer has a sugar house, and a fine grove of maple trees, and glittering tin sap buckets hang on all the trees; and instead of a large iron kettle for boiling the sap, evaporators have been installed, where the sap runs in thin and clear and comes out a beautiful light brown sirup.

Imagine the joy of little Oisette when she was allowed to go to a sugaring off with her little English neighbors. They drove off from the main highroad into a path in the woods where the runners of the sleigh sunk in deep slush and snow, and finally came to this tiny house in the heart of the wood. There was a fine wood fire under the evaporator, and from it steam was rising. The contents gave out a most delicious aroma.

Each child was given a spoon and a saucer, and in the saucer was poured about a cupful of boiling hot sirup; this fluid had to be stirred around and around fast and faster, until it thickened. When it was about the consistency of butter it was spread on slices of bread and eaten while it was still hot. Each child tried to see who could be ready first. The Dudley children were expert at it, and sang "Waltz me around again, Willie, around, around, around," as they stirred. Oisette felt shy with so many English children and would only say "Voilà" when her sugar was ready to be consumed.

Some of the older members of the party tried another method. They packed a pan full of clean white snow, gathered in the woods, and pounded it down very smooth and hard; on this was poured the very hot sirup, which formed at once into a sort of toffee, thin but clear and delicious to taste, but very chewey, somebody called it "The dentist's friend," because eating it is apt to loosen fillings in one's teeth.

Carleau, Monsieur Tremblent's dog, had arrived at the sugar house with the sleigh, and some one was unkind enough to give him a bit of this maple toffee. Poor Carleau, it glued his teeth tight together so that he could not bark, nor could he chew. The only thing he could do was to shake his head sadly from side to side and whine and whine and whine. This act made the whole party laugh in chorus, and dogs are very sensitive creatures, so when he discovered that this derision was directed toward him, he forsook the party altogether and trotted off home alone.

Later on in the afternoon, there came a time when the merrymakers themselves began to feel a little ill at ease, and longed to be off home and get a good drink of water. Then some one produced a big bottle of pickles and passed those about. Pickles never tasted so good before to any one as they did to that sugaring off party in the Canadian woods.

When the little girls were again in the big sleigh, ready to go home, each one was presented with a nice little cake of sugar, with escalloped edges. Oisette put hers carefully away in her treasure box. It was quite a long time before she cared to eat it: and as for Carleau, when he smelled sirup boiling in his master's kitchen, he fled out of doors.

It is marvelous to watch such a winter break up. The snow, which has planted its four feet deep in the city streets, is, of course, carted away on the main thoroughfares, so that the cars can be operated with the aid of sweepers and shovelers; but on the side streets when after a big storm the snow is piled in banks each side of the pavement, it is very like walking through a beautiful white tunnel, of course the tunnel has no top, and one is able to see the beautiful blue sky overhead, and to hear the jingle of many sleighbells, as no vehicle on runners is allowed to proceed without these bells.

The ice in the river, early in April, begins to crack and groan until suddenly on some sunny day, with a roar of sound, it piles itself high upon the banks. The melting snow on the hillsides runs down to meet it; the icicles, which have hung like white fringe everywhere, drop, drop, drop—like ripe fruit. Presently the double windows and storm doors are taken from off the buildings. The foliage on Mount Royal comes out a lovely green, the wooded hills are full of violets and trilliums, the latter is a three-leaved white lily, white and graceful, and when brought into captivity will thrive for a week if it has plenty of water. Summer comes on with a rush, and up the side of Mount Royal the elevator starts running for the season. Do you see the only springtime is when winter may be said to leap into summer!

CHAPTER V

A SIGHT-SEEING TOUR

One beautiful June morning, Miss Anstruther, the governess for the Dudley children, decided that she would like to take her pupils on a sight-seeing tour about the city of Montreal, so that their study of local history might become something more than dry facts and dates to be memorized.

When they boarded the "around the mountain" car, they were delighted to find Oisette Mary sitting beside her mother in one of the front seats. Her hair was braided extra tight and her cheeks shone with soap; otherwise she was her placid little self.

The Dudley children were in high spirits and they raced through the car to get seats near their chum. "We are to study with our eyes and ears to-day and not from books. Can't you come along with us?"

Finally Madame Tremblent was appealed to. She was on her way for a morning's shopping and she always went to The Bon Marche, kept by The Dupuis Freres, where all the clerks were French, and all the signs read in that language; she was armed with a long list of necessities for her growing family, and as Oisette was sadly in need of a hat she had been commanded to escort her parent thither.

When they reached the Mount Royal station, where every one must transfer east or west, Miss Anstruther, gathering from the look of appeal in the little French girl's eyes that she really would like to join the sight-seers, said to the mother, in her soft French accent, "If Madame would trust her little girl to me, I would select the hat at Goodwears Departmental, as we have a message there to change some boots for George; and I recently purchased these sailor hats the children are now wearing in their millinery department. She could wear the new hat home and I would have the heavy one sent out on the noon delivery." Oisette was wearing a purple felt hat adorned with a green bow and the day was warm.

Now, Madame Tremblent had herself longed to shop just once in the English part of the city, but the thought of going alone, lest she should not find persons who talked French, had prevented her from doing so. It came to her that if she let Oisette go just once in such good company, why, in a week or so the child could be her mother's guide and she would see for herself all the wonderful things she had heard her neighbors discuss as they walked home from mass each Sunday. So she drew from her petticoat pocket a huge wallet and thrusting a bill in Miss Anstruther's hand burst into a volley of French directed to her offspring to be attentive, to take care and not to be too late in returning home. Just then the tram for the east end appeared around the curve, and Madame was gone before the surprised governess could make any reply. The children tried to say it all over again—"Soyez exact chez moi," "Prenez garde and bon jour."

"Prenez garde means safety first," explained Miss Anstruther, "so I beg you all to keep with me, for Madame's advice was good, and here comes our car for the west end."

Even the milliner took an interest in little Oisette. "It is so unusual to see the two nationalities shopping together," she said. It did not take long to find a white sailor hat with a gold and white ribbon around the crown, a facsimile of the one Queenie was wearing; and the other errands being done, they set out for the Château de Ramezay in a cab. Their way lead down a steep hill, past The Windsor Hotel and Dominion Square. In this square Oisette found another statue to admire. This one was the bronze figure of a horse rampant and a figure of a Canadian soldier was holding the animal by its bridle. This statue is known as The Strathcona Horse and was erected in memory of the brave Canadian boys who fell in the South African war. The regiment was called The Strathcona Horse after Lord Strathcona, a very wealthy Scotch Canadian who financed it in 1898.

"Did he race his horses?" asked the little French girl, for horse racing was something she understood. This question made every one in the car laugh, and Oisette was glad when the car turned into "Rue Notre Dame" for here she was more at home and able to tell her little friends more about the narrow streets that lead down to the river; how it was possible in olden days to barricade each end of a narrow thoroughfare from the Indians; finally they passed her beloved Notre Dame church, and about a half mile further on they came to the Château de Ramezay.

Here they alighted and entered a quaint old gateway, flanked on each side by pyramids of ancient cannon and cannon balls. The door, with its curious knocker, stood open, and, entering, they found themselves in a low ceiled hall.

The history of this building is contemporary with that of the city for the last two centuries and so identified with past historical events that it has been preserved from vandalism of modern improvement and is a genuine relic of the old Régime in New France. Though only a story and a half high, the Norman turrets on either corner of the building add to its dignity, and the plaster walls (plastered over thick stone walls) have a rich yellow color, reminding one of an ancient vellum missal mellowed for centuries in a monkish cell.

In an old document still to be found in the archives of the St. Sulpician Order, it is recorded that the land on which this château stands was ceded to the Governor of Montreal in the year 1660, about eighteen years after Maisonneuve planted the silken Fleur-de-Lys of France on these shores. Somewhere about 1700 a part of this land was acquired by Claude de Ramezay, when he came from France as a captain in the army with the Viceroy de Tracy, and was for many years Governor of Montreal and held official court in the Council Chamber to the right of the entrance hall.

It was into this room that Miss Anstruther first ushered her party, another long low room now used as a museum of rare and very valuable relics of Canada's past. Everything is labeled by the Antiquarian Society which has this building in its keeping. There were buckles once the property of some gay French chevalier—there were bones of a young Indian maiden discovered when builders on the mountainside were excavating for a modern dwelling early in this century, even her wampum belt was there, and from it those versed in Indian lore were able to tell her age, her tribe and the fact that she had become Christianized.

Miss Anstruther instructed Queenie to read in French all the labels aloud and let Oisette translate for them; in this way they got on famously. On the left of the entrance is a salon where there is an old harpsichord, some very interesting old oil portraits of early French governors, and some curious candelabras and other furnishings of an early period. This salon was where Madame de Ramezay entertained her friends from France. How strange must these gayeties have seemed to the dweller of the wigwam as the lights from the château shone out into the night! Once, long, long ago, there was a garden in the rear of the château which reached to the very water's edge; so the sound of the dancing and the laughter must have carried out on the stream. Nowadays this land behind the château is filled with warehouses, and the view of the river gone for all time.

What a contrast to the burden-bearing squaws must have been the gay French women in their powder and patches and hair dressed a la Pompadour as they danced a minuet in their stiff brocades and sparkling jewels, to the sound of a harpsichord.

"Oh, fair young land of La Nouvelle France,

With the halo of olden time romance,

Back like a half forgotten dream

Comes the bygone days of the Old Régime."

Some visitor wrote those words in the visitors' book where every one is asked to inscribe his name.

After the children had absorbed the most important contents of these two rooms they were ushered down a long flight of stairs, ladder-like in their steepness, into the vaults of the château.

These vaults were once the kitchens and laundry of the great château, the fireplaces were so huge the children walked right into them.

They were shown old spinning wheels, old churns, a curious wooden bread-making machine and a mammoth brick oven, where twenty loaves of bread could be baked with one firing. So one gathers that not all who lived in this château were gay idlers after all.

The most interesting vault was one leading out of these kitchens, as it was inky black owing to its having iron shutters, closed over closely barred windows. This, it is said, was where the family, the guests and all the servants had sometimes to hide from the Indians. When news came that some hostile tribe was entering the city all the women and children would be sent "en bas" (below).

After the English had taken Canada from the French, this same château was occupied by Sir Jeffry Amherst in his British uniform, and it is possible that from his garden he looked out over the river toward St. Helen's Island and watched the smoke and flame arise from the fire when General de Levis burned his colors rather than let them fall into English hands.

Then again, in 1775, the Chateau de Ramezay was the headquarters of the Continental army of America, and Commissioners met in the council chamber to try and untangle affairs after Montgomery's siege of Quebec had failed.

Benjamin Franklin was one of this commission, and down in the old vaults he set up the first printing-press that Canada ever had, and he issued manifestoes to the people.

"So, you see," said Miss Anstruther, as they finally left this famous spot, "that one building has housed first the French, then the English, and for a time some famous Americans, and nowadays tourists from all nations come to see its contents. It is the grandest relic of an illustrious past, and now, when you take up your history books and find the names of some of these men and women, they will seem more like people to you."

They had a long trolley ride into the west end of the city again, for they wished to reach the Grey Nunnery on the stroke of twelve, noon, for at this hour visitors are admitted to the Chapel.

At last the conductor rang his bell, stopped the car and called out — "Guy — Gee — Guy" — you see, "Guy" is the name of the street on which this convent has a visitors' entrance. The French pronunciation sounds like "Gee," and as the conductor gives both French and English names when he calls the streets it made the children all laugh to hear "Guy — Gee — Guy — Grey Nunnery for you, Madame." This convent, so called from the dress of its community, was founded in 1692, when Louis Fourteenth granted power to establish general hospitals and other institutions for the relief of the sick and aged poor in different parts of the country. In a cemetery under the chapel lie buried the bones of some of the sisters who long ago came from France to found this order in a barren land — they have the heart of the first Mother Superior preserved in alcohol, but this is shown only to a devout few.

A fire destroyed their first building, but the present convent has stood as it is about seventy years and over the main entrance is the inscription — "Mon père et ma mère m'ont abandonne, mais le seigneur m'a recivelli." The governess read this aloud to her charges and then translated it into "My father and my mother may forsake me but the Saviour will receive me."

This building of massive gray limestone occupies a whole block and houses one thousand souls. There are tiny babes whose parents have deserted them, there are older boys and girls, orphans, there are sick and aged old men and women, there are one hundred nuns and ninety novices to do all the work. All these lives are regulated by the sound of a convent bell.

Exactly on the stroke of twelve noon, the chapel doors open and visitors are admitted. As soon as they are seated the nuns file in two by two, and recite the stations of the Cross in a low monotone. Often some nun with a very beautiful voice sings an anthem. When the service is over a diminutive sister remains behind as a guide to take visitors over the building; one who speaks French or English equally well.

It is all very clean, from the great kitchens with vats of pea soup boiling and the laundries filled with steam in the basement, to the very top of the building where there are play rooms for the tiny tots. Here some of the older children line up and sing for the visitors and are quite ready to receive coins or candies. There is one room where blind people are taught to read and to do bead work, it is interesting to watch them select the right shade of bead by simply feeling the end of the box which holds them.

In another room there are nimble fingers making wax flowers, weaving lace and doing embroidery.

The drug store was redolent with drugs and a young nun was busy filling prescriptions; she laughed very hard when Queenie exclaimed: "Why, I smell Gregory's mixture!" In a tiny room there was a dental chair, in which was seated a young orphan, and a nun was busy filling this child's teeth. Nobody was idle, even the very old men and women helped with the scrubbing of the floors and woodwork.

It was just one o'clock when they came out again at the Guy Street entrance, and Miss Anstruther said it was high time they had luncheon. So they went to La Corona Café on that same street, and there, in a delightful out of door garden, they sat at a small table with the lovely blue sky above them and flowers all about them, and a very attentive waiter. It is quite like a Parisian café. During their meal they chatted together about what they had seen, and asked eagerly about what was to follow.

"It is a puzzle to decide," said Miss Anstruther, "whether we had best go up on Mount Royal where from that elevation I could point out to you many historic spots of interest, including St. Helen's Island named after Champlain's wife, who was a French Helen somebody—and Victoria Bridge built when the late King Edward was a boy of eighteen and he came out here on a tour, and stopped to drive the last rivet in this bridge, and the location of Dollard's Lane, named from a brave young Frenchman who fought the Iroquois—or shall we go out to Lachine by trolley in time to take the boat over the rapids, that will bring us into the docks by supper time and out home a half hour later.

"I vote for whichever will have the most about Indians," said George, "we can see the Victoria Bridge when we travel any day." At this moment a party of French politicians entered the enclosure and Oisette's eyes dilated with amazement, "Mon père!" she exclaimed. Sure enough, it was Monsieur Tremblent, and he, too, was amazed to behold his little girl in a new white sailor hat. Miss Anstruther explained how Oisette happened to be with them, so he took a great interest in their plans, and after consulting with his party found he could put a motor car at Miss Anstruther's disposal; in this they could cover more ground in the city and be taken out to Lachine, then theparty could see the rapids and the car could be brought back to its owner at five o'clock, when he would be returning from the political meeting.

Their plans were soon made, and their first stop was to be on Sherbrooke Street just west of Guy Street, where behind huge gray stone walls, is situated the grand seminary of the Sulpician Order. Entering these grounds, they could see the huge building which houses four hundred or more students, all preparing for the priesthood, but one reason of their visit was to see the two stone towers in the grounds which were built in very early times and remain standing in an excellent state of preservation. One of these old towers was used as a chapel for the Indian mission and the other as a school. A tablet on the chapel tower bears the inscription "Here rest the mortal remains of a Huron Indian baptized by the Reverend Père de Brebeuf. He was, by his piety and by his probity, the example of the Christians, and the admiration of the unbelievers; he died aged one hundred years the 21st of April, 1690."

Miss Anstruther reminded George that he had but recently read in Parkman's history about this same Rev. Père de Brebeuf, who was tortured to death by the Iroquois with every cruelty devisable.

The school held in the other tower had, at one time, a famous native teacher; she was called "the school mistress of the mountains," and died in 1695, when but twenty-eight years old. Above the door of the western wing of the great seminary is the legend in Latin "Hie evangel; bantur Indi," "Here the Indians were evangelized."

Next they rode along Sherbrooke Street, past a beautiful art gallery and some fine residences to the McGill University grounds, which lie at the foot of the mountain slope. This college was founded in 1821 and named from its founder the Honorable James McGill. Then, just a little further on, is the Royal Victoria college for women, donated by Lord Strathcone, and a beautiful statue of Queen Victoria ornaments the entrance steps — this statue was designed by the Princess Louise, one of Queen Victoria's own children. Miss Anstruther said she hoped some day her little students would become McGill graduates.

As motors are not allowed on Mount Royal, it was decided that they would go out to Lachine by the lower road, in this way they passed very many interesting places. Near the Place d'Armes stood the house of Sieur du

Luth, from whom the city of Duluth was named, and west of St. Lambert hill was a tiny house once the home of Cadillac, who left the then little French village to proceed westward and found the now beautiful city of Detroit.

In the years which came after, such men as Washington Irving, General Montgomery, Benjamin Franklin, Benedict Arnold, John Jacob Astor all lived for some time in Montreal, and all had something to do with the making of its history. In many places the Antiquarian Society has marked the various sites where these famous men made their homes.

On this lower road to Lachine, and within hearing of the sound of the rapids, stands a very old windmill, said to have been built in 1666 when La Salle came to Montreal,—there are also crumbling remains of a fortified château nearby and there is a well-founded legend that the old chimney attached thereto was built by Samuel de Champlain himself in his trading post of logs. The snowflakes of three hundred winters have fallen into that great fireplace since those stones and mortar were laid.

The Lachine Rapids were first run by a steamer in the summer of 1840 by the side-wheeler Ontario—afterward this boat's name was changed to The Lord Sydenham—and for very many years an Indian pilot took the wheel and steered the course over treacherous rock and reef. From very early times these rapids had been navigated by Indians in their frail canoes, and they knew where the water was deep enough for a large boat to go.

George Dudley was keen to see the village of Lachine itself and seemed quite worried because everybody was alive and well, as he had but recently read in his history of the Massacre of Lachine, but he had forgotten that it happened in 1689. It was in the summer of that year that the Iroquois descended upon this little hamlet on a very dark night and surrounded every house at midnight, and then with terrible yells and war-whoops destroyed every house and killed every living being.

It was nearly five o'clock when the little party left their borrowed automobile and boarded the steamer to shoot the rapids—they got right in the bow of the boat and Oisette stood on a chair where she could see the flying spray.

Altogether, it had been a wonderful event in her life, for French Canadian children, as a rule, do not have a whole day's outing, and when at last she was home again and tried to tell her mother about it, the good woman crossed herself to think of the dangers her little girl had come through.

CHAPTER VI

A LITTLE TRAVELER

INDUSTRY is another trait which our little Quebec cousin has to her credit.

The interior of Oisette's home was filled with objects which go to prove this. For instance, all the bed clothes, with the exception of the sheets, consist of gay patchwork quilts. French Canadian children learn to sew patchwork when they are very young indeed. Oisette learned to put together red and blue and yellow and white cotton cubes, which were made into wonderful squares of patchwork, just as soon as she could hold a needle that some older person threaded for her. She could thread her own needle long before she knew how to tell what hour it was by the clock.

She knew that to have a quilt one must first make thirty-six of these squares. In the Tremblent household were not only quilts that had been pieced together by a great grandmother who had resided in Quebec City, but bedspreads made by a grandmother who lived across the river in a little village named Chambly, and many made by her own mother when she was a little girl.

Indeed, on Oisette's own bed was a quilt of marvelous pattern made by an aunt for whom Oisette was named. This aunt had since become a cloistered nun, and was shut in from the gay world and spent her time mostly in prayer!

The pattern was known as "The music of the spheres." It consisted of circular bits of red and yellow cotton, which looked like onions floating in a bright blue sky. Right in the center of the counterpane was a big purple star, the long points of this star were tipped with yellow cotton and reached right to the edge of the bedspread.

This comforter was used for the first time when little Oisette Mary was only thirty-six hours old. She was taken by her father and her aunt to the church to be christened; you know a French Canadian child is always christened within three days after birth, and when the tiny babe was put back in its mother's bed the wonderful quilt was spread over the foot of the bedstead and the proud father declared that the little one opened its eyes and noticed the lovely colors even then.

A few months later, when she was old enough to be put down on the floor, she showed a great fancy for the rag rugs, with their gay stripes. These rugs are called Habitant carpets, and are made by the industrious method of sewing together long strips of colored cloth, these strips are rolled into big balls, as large as one's head, and six of these balls, when woven with carpet thread, make a very pretty rug. Most of the convents have looms where they will weave these balls for a small sum of money per yard.

There is something very cheering about the interior of a French Canadian domicile. First of all, there is usually much clean paint, either yellow paint like the clearest sunlight or bright blue paint like a summer sky. Then the window panes sparkle with cleanness, and the window-sills are filled with flowering geraniums and fuchsias, the latter plant being a great favorite in the French Canadian home. These flowers are usually growing in tin cans, but the tin is always very bright and shining. Then the wall papers are never dull or dark in color. Often they are either designs of bright flowers or gold stars. The pictures on the walls are always of interest. First and foremost there is always a picture of the Pope. Then a picture of the Christ, and very often indeed one finds a picture of Madame Albani in all her diamonds and tiara as she appeared when she sung for Queen Victoria at Windsor Castle.

Albani, indeed, was a little Quebec cousin who became world famous. She was born at Chambly, near Montreal, in 1852, within sound of the roaring rapids of the River Richelieu, and in sight of the old historical fort. She was the oldest daughter of one Joseph Lajeunesse, who was a musician of sorts, playing the piano, the fiddle, the harp and the organ. Indeed, he played the church organ at Chambly for many years, and he taught singing in the Sacred Heart Convent at Back River. When little Emma Lajeunesse was twelve years of age, the family moved to Albany, New York, and she went to a convent school there, where her voice was discovered when she sang in the cathedral. It was the citizens of that city who made up a purse and sent her over to Italy to study music. And so out of gratitude she called herself Madame Albani. But when she became famous she returned to Montreal many, many times on concert tours, and was much loved by her own people there, who secured her picture to ornament their homes, and always speak of her as "The lady who sings better than the birds."

Dr. Drummond, who lived in the Province of Quebec, once wrote some delightful verses in the broken English of the Habitantfarmer, which lines describe hearing Madame Albani sing:

"Dat song I will never forget me,

'Twas song of de leetle bird,

When he's fly from its nes' on de tree top,

'Fore rest of de worl' get stirred.

Madame she was tole us about it, den start off so quiet an' low,

And sing lak de bird on de morning, de poor little small oiseau."

Then the last stanza goes like this—

"We're not de beeg place on our canton, mebbe cole on de winter too,

But de heart's 'Canayen' on our body an' dat's warm enough for true!

An w'en All-ba-nee was got lonesome for travel all roun' de worl'

I hope she'll come home lak de bluebird an' again be de Chambly girl!"

That, you see, is why the photograph of Madame Albani is given a place of honor in our little Quebec cousin's home.

There is one ornament also that is never missing from the French-Canadian interior, no matter how shabby the surroundings. There is always a crucifix, which teaches its lesson of sacrifice and love to all.

These people are a home-abiding race. They travel but little. If they have a fiddle and a pack of cards for amusement, they do not feel the lure of the moving picture theaters. Sometimes, if any of the family get ill, they will make a pilgrimage to the shrine of St. Anne de Beaupré. But very many of them never leave their happy homes for even one night.

Oisette was twelve years of age before she made her first long visit away from home. To be sure, she had been at the convent school for three years, but that was on the Island of Montreal, and one journeyed there by driving. But to go by night boat to Quebec one hundred and sixty miles away, that was traveling.

Just as the city clocks and church bells were sounding their seven o'clock duet, the big night boat for Quebec, known as the steamerRichelieu, swung out into mid-stream. The current of the river St. Lawrence is very rapid just here, opposite the city of Montreal.

On the rear deck Monsieur Tremblent was standing and his little daughter Oisette Mary was with him. The month was June and the weather was very beautiful indeed.

The little traveler gazed with rapture at the receding shores, bathed in a lovely sunset glow. Everything pleased her; she would like to have opened all the stateroom doors and taken a peep inside, but her father explained to her that this was not allowed, except stateroom number seventeen, for that he had a large key; and presently she could go to bed in the top berth, and watch the panorama of moving shore line from out the port hole. But she wanted to sit up as long as her eyes would stay open and watch the travelers ascend and descend the very grand staircase. Above the mirror, which one always finds on these river boats, just halfway up the staircase, was a full length portrait of Richelieu himself, in his gorgeous robes, and holding a scroll in his hand. Oisette tried hard to remember his name, and wondered if he had been a Pope! She would ask the good sisters at the convent when she had to return to her lessons.

Presently she discovered in the salon, a large glass counter, like in a shop, where all sorts of fancy goods were displayed for sale.

There were Indian baskets, picture post cards, and jewelry and candy. Her father told her she might buy a present to take to his mother who lived in the city of Quebec; she became so absorbed trying to discover what she could find that her grandmère would like that she never missed her father at all, she stood just where he had left her and gazed and gazed; while he was on the lower deck, having bought a cigar he stopped to chat with a commercial traveler from Ontario, who was much interested to hear about the melon farm; and followed Mr. Tremblent back again up the grand staircase, when he went to find his little girl.

Oisette had just decided upon an Indian basket for her grandmother. This basket was woven in green and pink straw and shaped like a melon. "It will hold her knitting," she explained. "And she will think of you when she sees the melon."

This amused the Ontario man, who shook hands with Oisette and asked her to help him pick out something for his little girl. Finally, after much looking, a pair of red slippers with bead work on the toes was purchased. Then the stranger bought a very tiny straw basket, which contained a thimble; the latter just fitted Oisette's finger, and she was made very happy when he told her she was to keep it.

She made one of her deep curtsies, as the nuns had taught her, and said softly, "Merci bien, Monsieur."

That phrase amused the giver so much that he took out his note book and wrote it down, and he asked her to spell it for him, and kept saying it over and over. "I'll tell my little girl," he said, "that these were your very words!"

Oisette showed her father the thimble and whispered to him, "I shall make him a quilt!" Her father laughed and repeated her saying to the stranger, who declared that the very next time he visited Montreal he would drive out to the melon farm and see how the quilt was coming on.

At last Oisette was ready to go to bed. It was quite late now, but Quebec has a long twilight in summertime, and from out the portholes she could see the little villages along the shore.

There was always a fine big church and a good-sized convent, and clustered about these were such tiny houses.

Finally, she fell asleep and dreamed that the big churches were large hens and the little cottages were chickens cared for by the very big hens on the hill! And sometimes they seemed to be all racing along the river's edge together.

CHAPTER VII

THE CITY OF QUEBEC

THE big steamer Richelîeu was moored at the docks below the historic city of Quebec at seven o'clock the next morning. Tourists were allowed to remain in their staterooms until eight o'clock if they chose and breakfast was furnished on board. But Monsieur Tremblent and Oisette were early risers and were among the first to walk down the gangplank, attend to their luggage and depart for the upper town, where Grandmother Tremblent would have a good breakfast of bacon and eggs ready for her guests.

They did not drive up the steep hills in a calêche, nor did they take the trolley, for Monsieur Tremblent knew of a short cut; he couldreach his mother's home more readily by walking one block in the lower town and then taking an elevator, which runs right up the side of the cliff and deposits its passengers on the Terrace, where the beautiful Château Frontenac stands.

Already Oisette felt as though she were walking in the pages of history: for she knew well the story of Samuel de Champlain, who had founded this city so long ago. How he made friends with the Algonquins and listened to their stories of rivers and lakes and boundless forests, and how with them as allies he led the French in many wars against the Iroquois, the most bloodthirsty of all Indian tribes; how he bore the welfare of his colony upon his heart to the very end, dying upon Christmas Day in 1635. He was buried close beside Fort St. Louis, which is now the site of the beautiful hotel, the Château Frontenac. This hostelry often shelters nowadays ten times the number of people who made up the population of New France, as Canada was called in the days when it was governed by the brave Champlain.

Think of it! At that date six white children represented young Canada, and Madame de Champlain had scarcely any companions of her own sex, save the three serving women who had come with her from France.

When the elevator deposited Monsieur Tremblent and Oisette Mary at the top of the cliff, a short flight of steps brought them to the Champlain monument, and here they paused to get the wonderful view of the St. Lawrence as it widens to the sea. Here Monsieur Tremblent had a fine opportunity to point out to his little girl many things of interest; on the opposite shore was Levis, and from there one gets a trolley along the river bank to the station where one can see the wonderful new bridge, which has the largest span in the world, and which crosses the river at such a height that the largest boats from over the ocean can sail beneath it.

The tin roof and spire of a great church rises on that bank also. It is the parish church of St. Romauld; this church contains very lovely mural paintings done by an Old World artist some seventy-five years ago. A wealthy priest spent all the money left by his mother's estate in importing a young artist who had just won a grand prize in Paris, and entertained him as his guest for three years, until the work was done, and his paintings are growing more mellow and beautiful as the years pass. Monsieur Tremblent had, as a small boy, been an acolyte in that very church, and so little Oisette gazed with rapture at the roof shining like a diamond in the morning sunshine.

Goodness knows she was hungry when Madame Tremblent's house, situated on the Grand Alley, was reached; she found that her grandmother, whom she had not seen for several years, had grown smaller and thinner and wore a black lace cap on her head, but that her eyes were as bright as ever, and she had such a happy contented smile of welcome for her son and her granddaughter, whom she kissed on both cheeks.

During the morning Oisette unpacked her belongings, and became accustomed to the tall, narrow, stone house, with its long flights of narrow stairs, its tall, narrow windows; a house where one had breakfast in the basement, with windows on the street level, and received one's visitors in a salon upstairs, a very grand room with lofty ceilings and heavy cut glass chandeliers that tinkled when any one walked heavily in the room above.

To go to her bedroom she had to climb another long flight of narrow stairs. But here, again, the view was so wonderful that she forgot to be homesick.

Her grandmother owned a marvelous big black cat with yellow eyes that answered to the name of Napoleon, and also a dog, another Carleau by the way, old and feeble now, sleeping most of his time away, but he managed to wag his tail slowly when he heard little Oisette Mary's voice.

In the sitting-room, which was bright with red curtains, flowered walls and much fancy work of colored worsteds, there was a very yellow canary in a very bright clean cage.

This bird had a very shrill little note that made one's ears flutter, and he sang from the time the church bell rang for early mass until nightfall. Sometimes when he became too shrill, Madame would take off her black apron and hang it over the top of the cage and bid the warbler to "marche a couché."

Oisette was very much amused at this camouflage. "It is the daylight saving bill for the pauvre oiseau," she explained to her father.

Monsieur Tremblent had much business to attend to on this trip, but he managed to have Oisette go with him to the Falls of Montmorency, where the river of that name takes a leap of two hundred and fifty feet and joins the St. Lawrence; and to visit the Duke of Kent's house. The Duke of Kent was the father of Queen Victoria of England, and about the house are growing the most lovely old-fashioned flowers. Then, one Sunday afternoon, they took a long ride on the trolley and visited the shrine of St. Anne de Beaupré. Even before they left the tram car, Oisette espied the stone basilica on the top of a very pretty green hill, and as they entered the village the chimes were ringing a processional and a number of cripples thronged through the pillared vestibule. This shrine is world famous and sufferers have come one thousand miles sometimes, to wait, like those of old in Bible days, for the moving of the waters.

When they were finally allowed inside the church Oisette gazed in awe at the pillars covered with cast-off crutches, which faithful pilgrims have left behind them as they have gone forth healed. Then she walked slowly down the church aisle with her father and saw the great statue in gold of the good St. Anne herself, and they were shown by the priest a sacred relic.

This is a small glass box and in it rests a bone which the faithful believe is the wrist bone of the dead Saint Anne herself. St. Anne was, you see, the mother of the Blessed Virgin Mary. Little Oisette knelt beside her father, and each was allowed to kiss the glass which held this relic. Doing this made them both feel very happy and good.

The history of this shrine of St. Anne de Beaupré goes back almost to the time of Samuel de Champlain himself. A traditional account of its foundation relates that some Breton mariners being overtaken by a very violent storm on the great St. Lawrence river knelt in their boat and prayed to the good St. Anne, and vowed to her a sanctuary if she would bring them safe to shore.

Their prayers were heard, the wind drove them ashore. So, high on this hill, they raised a little wooden chapel at Petit Cap and while they were engaged in its construction one of the men became the subject of the first miraculous cure. He was badly crippled with rheumatism, but as he worked on the building the pains all left him. Presently other cures followed and the shrine became renowned for miracles. It has been known for two and a half centuries. In that period it has been rebuilt many times over. The shrine that Oisette visited was built in 1886 and since that date has had over one hundred thousand pilgrims come every year to its healing altars.

Now, every one does not get cured. Some who are brought there on beds stay week after week, trying so hard to get help. Others arecured after just one visit, and go away so very grateful and happy.

Oisette and her father went through a museum at the rear of this "L'eglise de la bonne St. Anne," and saw, carefully put away in glass cases, the most wonderful jewelery — watches, rings, bracelets — left behind by visitors who had been helped, and who wanted to leave some expression of their gratitude. Just what good such baubles can do is a puzzling question. But the wanting to give them is what counts, isn't it?

One morning shortly before their return home, Monsieur Tremblent had business at the Château Frontenac, so he told Oisette if she would wait for him on the Terrace, he would afterward take her to see the Citadel, and then they would have a view of the Plains of Abraham.

This Terrace, known as Dufferin Terrace, is a lovely spot. There is a band concert about ten-thirty every morning, and the people walk up and down and laugh and chat. There are always children playing out in this sunny spot, watched over by nurse maids, or fond mammas. There are always many tourists who come and go from the Château, whose great doors open on this historic spot. So, for a long time, Oisette was contented to sit quietly on a bench and hear the music and watch the crowds. Mingling with the civilians were a good many soldiers and blue jackets, for there were several big ships at anchor in the harbor below.

Oisette didn't care for soldiers. You see, she belonged to a peace-loving people, and to her the greatest honor which could come to her family would be to have a sister a nun, or a brother a priest. But soldiers were men who killed people, and she couldn't understand why the throng on the terrace treated these uniformed visitors with such respect.

Presently a little girl about her own age, who was dressed all in white, and carrying a white and red parasol, came and sat down on her bench and smiled at Oisette. "Hello! aren't you the melon child?" she said. Oisette almost fell off from the bench in surprise. But she managed to nod her head. "Don't you remember me? I knew you at once. We have often gone out to your place after melons, but they said you were away at a convent. Did you run away from the convent? I am sure I should." As she talked, the newcomer moved along and held her parasol over Oisette's head.

This kindly act warmed our little Quebec cousin's heart. "Oh, no," she said, "I love the convent and the good sisters, but I am here visiting my grandmother."

"We are here," said the child, "with all the family, to stay until my brother Reggy sails away with his regiment. He is in camp now at Valcartier and we ride out to see him almost every day in the motor. I'll take you if you like, some day."

French Canadian children are seldom rude, and to say to this little Canadian girl who adored soldiers, that she, Oisette, didn't like them, would be awkward. At this moment the band struck up "God save the King" to mark the close of its morning concert; and the little visitor closed her parasol with a snap, stood at attention, and sang in her childish treble:

"God save our gracious King,

Long live our noble King,

God save our King.

Send him victorious,

Happy and glorious,

Long to reign over us.

God save our King."

And when that was over, Oisette saw her father approaching, so she hoped she would not have to say that she didn't care much about a ride to Valcartier. But little Miss Sage had no idea of forsaking Oisette; she was too delighted to find some one from home. So she also greeted Mr. Tremblent with joy.

"'ARE YOU GOING TO THE CITADEL IN ONE OF THOSE FUNNY CALÊCHE THINGS?'"

"Oh!" she said, "are you going to the Citadel in one of those funny calêche things? I am crazy to ride in one. I want to go in one that has a yellow lining. Father says I would look like a fried egg if I got into one of that color." Monsieur Tremblent had always liked this little girl when she visited his farm, so he said: "If you will get permission from your people, you shall ride with us this morning. We will be three fried eggs."

While Monsieur Tremblent was making a bargain with a calêche driver, little Helen Sage was rushing about the Hotel Frontenac to find some of her family and leave word with them where she was going. At last, having found all the bedrooms empty, she went to the desk and wrote on a telegraph blank,—"Have gone to the Citadel with the Melon family. Yours,

Helen." This she tucked under her mother's bedroom door, and with a light heart skipped out to join her little friend.

When you come to think of it, both these little girls are little Quebec cousins, so it is like having two heroines to a story! Oisette knew well the early history of this wonderful walled city. The French achievements, and the names of the early Jesuits who suffered and worked among the Indians. And Helen Sage knew well the English side of the story: how General Wolfe had climbed with his army up the steep cliff and surprised Montcalm on the Plains of Abraham and captured all of Canada for the English. So Monsieur Tremblent found it very interesting to listen to their comments as they walked about inside the picturesque Citadel. Helen knew the age and history of the chain gate by which they entered. She knew, too, which of the cannon had been captured by the British at Bunker Hill. She patted it and said: "It is the nicest cannon here, isn't it? Father says, 'They have the hill but we've got the cannon'!"

The result of this trip was very interesting. Helen insisted on taking Oisette in their motor the next morning all over the city of Quebec, until she knew every bit of it externally. The St. Louis Gate, named by Cardinal Richelieu after his Royal Master, Louis XIV of France; the Dufferin Gate, named from one of the earlier Governor Generals of Canada, the Earl of Dufferin, a most popular Irishman, who helped blend the two nationalities in a wonderful manner. A fascinating old curiosity shop in an old house that was once the town house of the Duke of Kent. She pointed out all the tablets and the headquarters and the graves of the famous warriors of olden times. And, in her turn, Oisette took Helen to see "Notre Dame des Victories," the oldest church in this country, built as Champlain directed. She showed her the sign of the Golden Dog, and read to her the inscription:

"Je suis un chien qui ronge l'os

En le rongeant je prends mon repos,

Un jour viendra, qui n'est pas venu,

Que je mordrai qui m'aura mordu."

Translated this reads:

"I am the dog that gnaws his bone

I crouch and gnaw it all alone,

A time will come, which is not yet,

When I'll bite him by whom I'm bit."

There is a tablet in gold on a plain bare frontage. A dog gnawing a bone, the dog is couchant (lying down), the bone is that of a man's thigh-bone! Madame Tremblent had told Oisette the interesting legend of Le Chien D'or. It had its origin in the mercenary practices of the last Intendant of Quebec under the French régime — Intendant means a "City Manager" of modern times. This wicked one's name was Bigot. At a time when food was very scarce indeed, and ships from France bringing provisions to her colony were delayed by wind and weather, Bigot gathered from poor farmers all the grain and food stuffs he could lay hands on and stored them in a building close to his palace, and when the time was ripe and a famine at hand he planned to sell back all this food to the poor farmers who had raised it, and to charge them a very big price. The building where he stored all his goods became known as La Frippone — "The cheat."

Now, among the merchants of Quebec at that time was a man named Nicholas Jaquin, he was rich and yet he was generous. He had also a great warehouse on top of Mountain hill, where the Quebec post office now stands. He decided also to gather grain and foodstuffs and to sell them at the lowest possible price to the poor. Naturally, when the Intendant found he was being undersold he was very angry, he tried in every way to punish his enemy, who over his door put this sign of the Golden Dog, and the people all understood, but were afraid to show too much sympathy, as Bigot had been appointed by the King of France.

Finally, the Intendant caused his enemy to be slain in the streets of Quebec — the actual assassin escaped for a time, but the murdered man's son tracked him to far off Pondicherry and struck his father's slayer down — the story ends there.

They also visited the Ursuline Convent, which has associations artistic and martial as well as religious.

There is a votive lamp, lighted one hundred and seventy years ago by two French officers, who came to attend the ceremony of their two sisters taking the veil, which means that these young ladies became nuns and never lived outside the convent walls again.

That lamp was to be kept burning forever—it was out for a short time during the siege of 1759; then it was relighted, and for well over one hundred years was never dimmed.

This chapel also contained paintings sent over from France for safe keeping at the time of the French Revolution; and generally supposed to be by great artists, such as Vandyke and Campana; but even though they may be but copies they are very well worth seeing.

The great General Montcalm was taken to this convent to die, and was buried within the precincts in a grave dug for him by a bursting shell.

They also went to the Champlain market and to the Convent of the Good Shepherd, where the nuns dress always in white, and never cease their prayers day nor night; every six hours they change vigils, but always, always, there are some of them there before the altar, and one each side of the steps of the high altar.

Grandmother Tremblent took a great interest in this friendship, though she did not always appear in person she directed many of the excursions and answered all of Oisette's questions.

The very first day Oisette arrived she had asked about Richelieu, and almost every day thereafter she had learned some new fact; she had a good memory, and when she got back home she would remember to tell her mother about the great boat by which she had traveled, and the picture, life-sized, of the Cardinal in his red robes, who had been Minister of State during the reign of King Louis XIV of France; in fact Grandma had said he was the true founder of the city of Quebec, for in 1627 he had revoked the Charter of De Caen, a Huguenot merchant, and had organized a company of one hundred associates, himself the head. The colonists were to be given lands and were to send all their furs to France and France was to send food to them, so that they would not have to do much farm work, but made fur peltries their sole industry. It was a niece of the great Cardinal Richelieu who by her charity and her gifts founded some of the early societies that existed in the city of Quebec.

On the last day of Oisette's stay with her grandmother, Helen Sage came for tea in this quaint old house and admired Napoleon, the canary and the fancy work. She was pleased, too, with the quaint old furniture; a prie-dieu chair in Oisette's bedroom particularly took her fancy, the seat of this chair was very low, not more than a foot from the ground, and when lifted up revealed a little shelf for devotional books, and a devout person could kneel on this seat, facing the back of the chair, and the top of the chair back was made flat and wide to hold the open book.

In the dining-room was a beautiful mahogany sideboard. "Oh, please, has it a history?" asked Helen. "It is very ancient, my child," Madame answered. "In fact it was for years stored in my grandfather's barn under some hay, left there by an English officer who was recalled home. He told my people that some day he would come for it, but he never did, and at last the old barn was to be torn down, so my father gave the furniture to me."

There was also a glass cupboard, and desk, but all that Madame was inclined to say about them was that they were ancient—very ancient.

Some years ago, collectors of the antique went thoroughly over the Province of Quebec, and, where it was possible, purchased the best examples of furniture and china and ornaments, which had been brought from France by the old Régime. The furniture of that day was the most magnificent of all the French period. A few examples of the work of Andrew Boule found their way to the New World. He was the King's Cabinet Maker and was a great ebonist (a worker in ebony) inlaying his work, gilding it, bronzing it—anything to make it very splendid.

When tea was over, Grandmother Tremblent told them the story of Madeleine Verchères. Most of the historians and the novelists and the poets of Canada have told and retold this true tale of a little French Canadian girl of fourteen, who was left one summer day with her two brothers in the care of two soldiers and one old man, while her father, the Seigneur of Verchères, journeyed to Quebec.

Madeleine was out on a hillside gathering wild strawberries when she heard a shot ring out far down the valley and going to the top of the hill her young eyes could see a band of Iroquois riding swiftly over the plain toward her father's fort. So she sent the two soldiers to the block house to guard the women and children of the estate, then she and her brothers under cover of the dusk prepared dummies and placed them behind the walls; then, to further deceive the savages, she and her brothers patroled the fort through the night and called out "C'est bien," (All is well) so that the Iroquois supposed the fort to be fully garrisoned, and though they lingered about for a time they did not dare attack.

The next morning her father returned, and having learned that savages had been through the valley, brought a party of soldiers with him, expecting to find his home in ruins and his children kidnapped; instead of that a tired, hungry group of children greeted him with "C'est bien."

"So, you see, heroism was not confined to the men alone," said Grandmother Tremblent. "It was as it is now in modern days, the women and even young girls who must be very brave."

CHAPTER VIII

AT HOME

FINALLY the day came when Oisette must say good-by to Quebec, to grandmother, to ancient Carleau, to Napoleon, to the yellow canary, and then pay a last visit to the Terrace, and say good-by to everything there. The lovely view, the harbor boats, the statue of Champlain, the beautiful Château Frontenac, the band, and last, but not least, to the little Sage girl, who had been so friendly to her.

All these things would soon be memories, banked in her mind forever and ever. Monsieur Tremblent and Oisette returned to Montreal by rail, leaving the ancient walled city soon after the noontime, and, journeying back by a fast express, they reached the Place Vigerrailway station at six o'clock. Oisette proved to be a very good traveler. She enjoyed the view, she did not jump down from her seat and tear about as some other children were doing, but sat as her father had told her, and counted or tried to, the trees as they flew past. Sometimes she hummed softly her favorite song:

"Alouette, gentille Alouette, Alouette Je te plumerai,

Je te plumerai la tête, Je te plumerai la tête,

O Alouette, gentille Alouette, Alouette Je te plumerai."

A very pleasant surprise was when they reached Montreal, and her father decided to stop at the Place Viger Hotel for a meal before they should take the trolley home. For, to tell the truth, Oisette was very hungry indeed, and so was her father.

Presently they were seated at a little table out on a beautiful stone balcony, with pretty striped awnings, potted plants, where there was an orchestra of young ladies, all dressed in white, who played delightful music. The young lady at the piano kept smiling at Oisette. It was a new experience for our little Quebec cousin to have a full course dinner, served so beautifully, and to have pink ice cream. Do you know that ice cream is almost unknown in a Habitant home? To be sure, French children on the streets of Montreal have recently acquired "the ice cream cone habit"; but vendors of these sweets do not peddle their wares out in the country. Oisette ate her dessert slowly, her dark eyes followed the waiter as he came and went, and now and then she would glance over at the pianist.

When the meal was finished and they were about to depart, to her great surprise, as they passed near the piano, she heard a voice say, "Bon soir, Oisette." Monsieur Tremblent stopped, too, and shook hands with several of the musicians; and Oisette gasped with surprise,for one of them was a cousin of Oisette's mother. This orchestra was composed originally of the members of one family. Five sisters all trained by the nuns at the Sacred Heart convent. In three years' time three of the sisters had married and in each case the gap had been filled by another pupil from this same convent. They were still known as the five sisters, and they still dressed exactly alike. The one who had addressed Oisette was the newest member of the little company. Only the winter previous, at the convent, our little Quebec cousin had played a duet with this Mlle. Archambeau, and had done her part so well that one of the nuns had said to her, "We shall hear of our little Oisette on the concert stage some day."

During the five minutes' rest accorded this hotel orchestra these girls chatted like magpies with the travelers, and sent messages to the other members of the family, and said they hoped to get out to the melon farm some day during the summer, and warned Oisette that she must practice well on the piano, so that she might some day play another duet with her friend. Then the leader tapped his baton and the voices ceased. But the cousin whispered to Monsieur Tremblent: "We are going to play 'The Rosary' now. You'll hear it as you go down in the elevator."

When the-round-the-mountain car stopped at Cote-des-Neiges that night, Monsieur Tremblent and his little daughter alighted in the dusk. They planned to surprise the household. By crossing a meadow they approached the house from the rear, and thought it would be great fun to slip into the kitchen in the darkness and leave their parcels, and then perhaps take off their wraps. Oisette wondered if she might manage to be discovered playing the piano. The French Canadian loves a practical joke.

But it happened that some one in a motor car passed the trolley in which the returned travelers were journeying and the motor stopped at the

Tremblent farm about ten minutes before the car was due, and, of course, the visitors said whom they had seen. So Madame Tremblent was ready with every room lighted, and doors open, and Carleau was barking his head off with excitement. The Dudley children were tearing up the road, calling out, "Welcome home!" On the stove was a big pot of pea soup very hot, and on the table a big bunch of field daisies, which the Dudleys had brought early in the day. The big parlor lamp with its red shade was lighted, which meant that it was a very special occasion. Everybody gazed in surprise at Oisette. She certainly had grown a little taller, and she had a nice little manner, which quite unconsciously she had acquired from her grandmother. She forgot her shyness and told them everything; from the time she had left home until to-night when she had dined at the Place Viger. No pea soup to-night, thank you!

When at last she went to bed she gazed about her own room with a new interest. The room seemed smaller than she had thought it before, but her pictures were so pretty. Nowhere had she seen anything she liked as well as her Joan of Arc banner wrought in silk. And there was her own bedspread again, "the music of the spheres," placed there in honor of her return.

"Chime, chime, chime, chime," rang the church bell next morning. This was the bell that had awakened our little Quebec cousin since her birth. It sounded like an old friend, but what a funny, feeble little bell it was after the great tongues of the Quebec bells to which her ears had become attuned.

Presently she heard the popping noise of firecrackers, and Carleau barking madly in the door yard: and she remembered that it was July first, Dominion Day, a legal holiday all over the great country of Canada since 1867. There would be no work done by the English, and the trolley cars would bring numerous picnic parties out to the countryside: and the Dudley family were going to have great doings. They had tried to tell her about it last night, but her mind was still centered on Quebec.

By the time she had finished her breakfast and was out in the morning sunshine, she gazed with rapture at the Dudley's house. First of all, the

Union Jack was flying from a tall flag staff, then the piazza was draped with red, white, and blue; all the posts were wound with red, and strings of Chinese lanterns were dancing in the wind. She was told that there was to be a children's party and she was to come over to it, and they would like her to sing a little song, as there was to be an entertainment with the piazza for a stage. "You are to sing in French. Our governess says that will make a pleasing variety," explained the children.

"Here is what I am to recite," demonstrated Queenie Dudley, making a deep bow toward Oisette:

"Four fingers, a thumb, on each little hand;

Make five jolly holidays all through the land,

Victoria Day comes first, Dominion Day with its noise,

Then Thanksgiving and Christmas for girls and for boys,

Then comes the New Year, brimful of good cheer,

Merry Christmas to all and a Happy New Year."

"But that is not suited to the summertime," objected her brother. "Father taught you that for a Christmas party. You should have learned a new one by this time."

"Bosh," said young Queenie, "you always recite the same old thing, every party we have or go to. You just make your bow and say:

"Speaking pieces. What's the use, I'd like to know?

Getting up before so many when it scares a fellow so!"

Presently the piano was moved close to the window, and the governess played some tunes and told the children to let her hear them sing.

They all joined in with a will, and sang "The Maple Leaf, the Maple Leaf Forever"; and "Oh, Canada." When they had sung this once through in English, she coaxed Oisette Mary to repeat it alone in French, which she did in a very winning manner. All day long on Dominion Day these children romped together. Oisette felt it was good to be home with her dear little neighbors again; and when at last, tired out after the party, she went home and nestled down in her little bed she said an extra little prayer of gratitude to Our Lady for giving her such a happy first day home, and then, tucking the rosary under her pillow, she was soon asleep.

Oisette, like so many little French Canadian girls who are convent trained, will become proficient with her needle, she will play the piano, she will always greet one with a pretty bow and a soft shy voice should one come to visit her in this wonderful great land of Canada.

The Province of Quebec is not all French, there are little girls with a Scotch accent, and there are those with an English accent, and in Ontario there are those very like American children. But perhaps the French Canadian child with her quaint little ways in her humble home proves far the most interesting to the traveler, and her simple life teaches every one who knows her a lesson of obedience and contentment.

"Chime-Chime-Chime-Chime" — yes, the story ends here, but the bells still call and call little Oisette to awake, to come to prayers, to attend vespers — "Chime-Chime-Chime-Chime."

Our little Quebec cousin bows her head when she hears them "Chime-Chime-Chime-Chime" — and life goes on.

THE END